THE BABOON AT THE BALL

THE TRENGROUSE BALL
BOOK FOUR

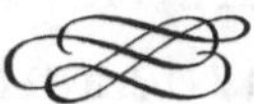

ELIZABETH LEYDIN

IMPROBABLE FICTIONS

ISBN 978-1-7635241-6-3

Improbable Fictions
PO Box 283
Annandale NSW 2038
Australia
contact@improbablefictions.com

THE TRENGROUSE BALL

The Trengrouse Ball…one magic night in a Cornish summer. Music, dancing, flirting and laughter. And deception, abduction, love and loss. New attractions, new hopes, and old flames rekindled. For some, a culmination. For others, a new beginning.

The Trengrouse Ball series follows the lives and loves of the Trengrouse family: eight grown children of the Earl of Trengrouse, each of whom is searching for the life they need; each battling their own fears but hoping for happy ever after.

After the Trengrouse Ball, their lives will never be the same again…

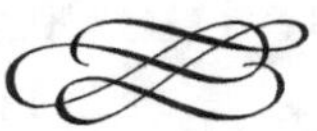

CHAPTER 1

"Mama says that once you appear at this ball, you will be "out", but not ready to marry," Melissa observed, a slight crease between her brows. "I thought "out" meant on the Marriage Mart."

She sat at Kerenza's small dressing table and opened her notions box. They were sharing a bedroom; the house would be full of ball guests for the next few days. The first ones were due to arrive any moment. Her oldest sister Demelza, a recent widow, had arrived yesterday, complete with her twin daughters and their governess, but she didn't count.

Kerenza grinned at her sister. Melissa did love to have things clear in her head. "When I get to London for the Season, then I'm really "out"—once I've made my curtsey to the queen. My ball is the first step. Mama, though, believes a girl should have at least one Season before she thinks of marriage. To bring her up to snuff."

"I was glad of that," Melissa said, the need for an explanation satisfied. "I have no wish to marry any time soon." She began to plait the thick ribbons she was planning to use as a sash on her ballgown.

"*I* do! When one is married, one has independence!"

"One has a lord and master, you mean."

"Oh, pooh! If one chooses correctly..."

Melissa gave her a strangely sad smile. "What is "correctly"?"

"A man who is dashing and kind and handsome and rich! And with a title, obviously," she added. "I'd like at least an earl.

Wouldn't you? Most of the dukes are old, and there are so few marquesses. But there are *lots* of earls. Surely one of them will propose?"

Melissa raised an eyebrow, but didn't say anything. She simply went back to her plaiting.

What a pretty sash it would be! Three different greens, and the dress was to be in Pomona green, which would suit Melissa's fair complexion and dark hair.

White was so boring! Kerenza wished she could wear deeper colours. Pale pinks and yellows washed her out. Secretly, she yearned for a deep blue dress, to highlight her eyes, but debutantes wore white at their first ball. Or something very pale.

Ah well, needs must. She examined her new long white satin gloves with satisfaction. Her first true pair of evening gloves, for her very first ball. At eighteen! She knew girls who had been out since they were sixteen. Her parents were so staid.

One night before she was a proper young

lady. She bit back a rueful smile. All of Mama's lectures had failed to make her proper. She would *try*, though. An earl's wife had to be proper. This ball was the *ton*'s first glimpse of her as an adult, and she *had* to make a good showing! Half of Cornwall and quite a few London guests were coming, and her success at her first Season would depend on their impression of her tomorrow night— and, for the guests who were staying, over tonight and the next few days.

A grumble of gravel under carriage wheels. Kerenza flew to the window and peeked out; she couldn't be seen spying on their guests for the ball. It was a luxurious coach, with wheels picked out in yellow and the top packed with luggage, but it had no crest on the door panel…

"It must be Mr Muffet," she said, disappointed. Trengrouse Hall would be full of noble guests for her birthday ball, but Mr Muffet was merely a business partner of her father. A widower, with one son, Percival, whom he was bringing to the ball. A Cit, of course, but her father's friend. The son had been at Cambridge until last year, Mama had said, so he must be presentable, at least.

She had a very vague memory of them coming to visit when she'd been in the nursery. So, before he'd been sent off to school. He'd run wild with the boys, of course. He'd be…what, Felix's age? Twenty-one or -two?

Something moved on the top of the coach. Good Heavens, it was a-an *animal*. Had some poor dog been left to travel all alone without any concern for its safety? That was monstrous!

The brownish ball of fur unfolded and a dark-muzzled face turned up to hers while a tail curved around a bag. A *monkey!* They had brought a *monkey!* Oh, perhaps the monkey was a birthday present for her!

What fun!

Still, she'd have to have words with Mr Muffet about letting the poor animal travel up there, alone and no doubt frightened.

Melissa had finished braiding. "Who is it?" She stood up, arranging her skirts neatly. Kerenza always felt like a positive shag-bag next to her. Who had time for neatness when there was so much going on?

"The Muffets."

Melissa's face lit up. "Excellent. Mr Muffet promised to bring me the newest edition of the almanac of moons and tides."

"Never mind that, they've brought a *monkey*!"

Kerenza turned back to the window, just in time to see the monkey leap athletically from the coach top to the ivy which ran up the walls, as the elder Mr Muffet climbed down the steps and Father came out to greet him.

Neither noticed the monkey.

"Oh, my word!"

She had to get that monkey before Father saw it! He'd never let it run free on the estate. If she didn't get it safely corralled, he'd say she couldn't have it.

Kerenza ran as fast as she'd ever run—at least, as fast as she *could* run, now she was in long skirts—out of the bedroom, down the stairs: one flight, two, three.

Father and Mr Muffet were in the hall. She changed course with a gulp and headed down the servants' stairs, coming out in the kitchen and banging straight into the scullery maid.

"Miss Kerenza!" the cook scolded.

She tossed a "So sorry!" over her shoulder and went out the back door, through the scullery and into the stable yard, then round the house widdershins until she came to the front steps.

The son was supervising the removal of their luggage from the coach.

"Mr Muffet!" she gasped. He turned, and for a moment she was distracted. He must be quite close to her age, she knew, but he seemed older. And very well dressed. A Pink of the Ton, if he hadn't been a Cit.

Those Hessians were blinding where the sun hit them.

He wasn't handsome, and nowhere near as tall as her brothers, but his face had something to it. She wasn't sure what; but although he barely had a nose at all, he wasn't ugly.

A perfect bow, too. She curtsied, habit taking over. "I'm afraid you have the advantage of me," he said.

"Oh, I'm Kerenza Trengrouse."

He bowed again. "Lady Kerenza. I've met your other sisters in London, and you resemble them in beauty." He smiled, but it was gentle rather than flirty, and he looked a little nervous. "It's an honour to meet you."

He drew breath to keep going with the pleasantries. "Felicitations–"

"Yes, never mind that. The monkey got away!" She pointed up at the ivy, where the animal was still clinging, apparently calm, surveying the scenery.

His gaze followed her gesture, and he said something under his breath.

"How did that get here!"

"On the top of your coach. Didn't you mean to bring it?"

"Bring it! I should say not." So it *wasn't* for

her. What a shame. "That animal's been nothing but trouble since Prinny gave it to us."

Why on Earth would the Prince Regent give the Muffets a monkey? A sign of Royal favour? It was very odd, even for Prinny.

"What did you give him in return?" she asked, considerably curious. What would be thought an appropriate gift? Of course, it being the Prince Regent, it would have to be something expensive.

"I'm sorry?" He was distracted by the question, but surely he'd thought of it before?

"If the Regent gives one a gift, one must give something in return." Surely everyone knew that? Yet Mr Muffet looked shocked.

The monkey hooted at them, and he frowned up at it, waving the question aside.

"I've got to get it down," he said. "Before it disturbs your family. I beg of you, don't tell Father it's here. I was supposed to make sure that it was safe and sound before we left."

He sounded troubled. Mr Muffet was a

kind man, but a stern father. And he held the very considerable purse strings.

"Why didn't you?"

"I thought I had." He concentrated on the monkey, as if willing it down. It ignored him. "I need fruit. I don't suppose you have any bananas?"

"*Bananas?*" No-one ate bananas. Why would they? The red fruit were stodgy and unappetising, although she had once had a banana fritter which was crispy and nice once salted.

"They've been the best thing to entice her down. Berries will work, though."

"We have strawberries. I'll get some."

Back around the house and into the kitchen.

"Mrs Lovell, could I have some strawber-ries, *please?*"

"What mischief are you about, Miss Keri?"

"None at all! I'm trying to *stop* mischief!" Monkeys were mischievous, weren't they?

The cook didn't seem to believe her, but

Joe the scullion shyly handed her a bowl of strawberries. She smiled dazzlingly at him, and ran back.

But when she arrived at the front steps, neither Mr Muffet nor the monkey were anywhere to be seen.

CHAPTER 2

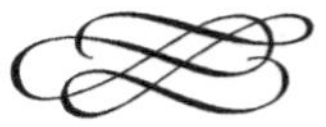

Percival hated this baboon. Hated it.

She was like an old fox: wily and cunning and far too smart for an animal. He took off his hat and tilted his head back to get a better look at her.

There she was, grinning down at him and hooting, clinging to the ivy as securely as if she were sitting in a chair.

Why the Prince Regent had given his father a baboon, God alone knew. His father had no idea. A gift from the Regent was *supposed* to be a sign of royal favour, and it was true they'd applied for Letters Patent for their tin manufactory, since they supplied the Army with a good deal of its eating and cooking equipment, and wanted to safeguard the innovative enamelling process his father had invented. It was much longer-lasting than the German version.

Was the baboon a sign that Prinny was well-disposed towards the idea?

And *had* Papa given the Regent a gift in return? Would Papa have known that etiquette. The thought that they'd been inadvertently rude made his stomach twist.

At the thought, he lost his concentration, stopped staring at her, and the bloody animal screeched and leapt, right over the carriageway and onto the lawn which stretched in all directions.

Lord, it was fast!

Percival took off after it, thankful for all the days he'd spent tramping over his friends' fathers' fields, pretending to shoot birds as a gentleman should; at least his wind was good.

The baboon headed for a copse of trees by a stream, to the right of the main drive. She liked to get high; perhaps she felt safer. How in damnation's name had she got onto the coach? He'd *locked* that stallion stall! The cook's boy was supposed to feed her through the iron bars which went from the chest-high oak partition to the ceiling. The boy must have opened the door.

His boots weren't made for running in, and his valet would have his head for getting them so dirty. But the trees were close, and he glimpsed the baboon leap into an oak tree.

Oh, no. Last week she'd got hold of un-ripe acorns, and it had upset her stomach in a terrible way...the *smell*...

He had to get her down. If only Lady Kerenza had brought the strawberries in time!

No, that wasn't fair. She had positively run to the kitchen, despite running being forbidden to young ladies.

Percival slowed as he reached the oak,

smiling involuntarily at the thought. Kerenza Trengrouse hadn't given the impression of a proper young lady. She was beautiful, though, and would probably set London alight when she made her come-out.

He'd been lucky it had been her, and not one of the more starched-up Trengrouses. Locryn, the eldest son, for example. He was stiffly polite, but very aware of his rank, which made Percival sharply conscious of his lower social position. The next few days would be a trial; having to perform to the *ton* who would all be looking down at him and his father, no matter how *kindly* they smiled at him. Lord, he hated that condescending kindness!

He had to make this visit a success for his father's sake.

His father was determined to make a man of the *ton* out of him, and any deviation from the strictest rules of society were treated like a mortal sin. Father had even made him read etiquette manuals meant for young women, so he'd know what they would expect of him!

He had to show that all the money and energy Father had poured into his education had been worth it. He might not be a nobleman, but he could act the gentleman. Once he got this bloody animal locked up.

THIS WAS NOT A GOOD TREE. The bark was scratchy and it had those hard little fruits which made her sick. But at least she was off the ground and could look down on the-man-who-locked-her-up.

He was searching for her. Hah. He tried to be the troop leader, but she knew better. The older man was his troop leader. They smelt alike, so they were family. He was just the junior, with no power. She would not obey him.

He kept looking. She would let him find her. He wouldn't climb this tree to get her. He always made other people do that, and he was alone.

She chittered insults at him.

Let him come close enough, and she would show her scorn.

THE BABOON CLUNG grimly to the branch, chittering at him. What he needed was a net.

Cornwall had an abundance of fishing boats. Surely there'd be a net somewhere on the estate?

The problem was, he couldn't take his eyes off the animal or she'd escape. A monstrous vision of her riding on one of the earl's prize sheep, as she'd done to his father's deerhound only last week, made him wince.

Perhaps Lady Kerenza would find them. If the lawn hadn't been so well kept, they would have left a trail, but it was shorn smooth. He might be stuck here all night, while his father animadverted to the Earl about his wild ways and incompetence.

Total libel. Compared to his fellow students at Cambridge, he'd been a pattern card of good behaviour. That was one way he *didn't* act like a gentleman. No carousing or wenching.

The baboon hooted. He held out his arms to the animal and made crooning noises.

"Come on, missy, come on down…"

Not a chance. That animal despised him, he was sure.

The problem was, his father wanted him to act as if he were fifty instead of twenty-two. It was only through brandishing the *Ackerman's Repository* magazine that he'd convinced his father that pantaloons were *à la mode*, and only older men wore knee breeches during the day.

It wasn't *easy* to know about fashion when one hadn't been born to it. His father couldn't advise him. His friends at university —he shuddered to think of how they'd have ragged him should he have asked. It was all observation, research and employing a top-flight valet and tailor.

As if encouraged by that thought, the baboon pissed straight down onto him. He ducked fast enough to escape it on his face, but the foul liquid sprayed right across his shoulders. On his new Bath superfine! The baboon laughed—he would *swear* it was laughing—and jumped right into the next tree while his head was down.

By the time he turned around to look, she had disappeared.

He *hated* the blasted thing!

HEHEHEH.

CHAPTER 3

Kerenza felt rather foolish, standing in the forecourt with a bowl of strawberries while the footmen unloaded the Muffets' luggage.

Where could they have gone?

Bryok, one of the footmen, said over his shoulder. "If you're looking for the young gentleman, he took off into the copse like the hounds of hell were after him."

She grinned, and then pulled her face into repose. Really, Bryok needed to learn some decorum! He'd grown up on the estate, though, and was one of her brother Ives' cronies.

So they'd gone to the oak copse. Unusual to coppice oaks, but Father was doing it for the boatbuilders in Swain Cove. He was letting the ones on the house side grow tall, though, to give a better outlook from the library.

She set off across the lawn, careful to avoid the sheep droppings. The flock had been all over here yesterday, getting the lawn in a fit state for visitors, and the gardeners' boys hadn't been yet to gather the dung for their muck heap.

It struck her, for the first time, how many interlocking activities were necessary to create an estate like Trengrouse Hall. How intertwined the Hall was with the lives of locals—not only the ones on the estate, but further afield, in nearby villages. She'd never properly considered it before, although of course she *knew* about it all. Perhaps Mama was right, and she wasn't ready for marriage. The thought of presiding over a place like this made her nervous; not a feeling she often had.

Grateful for the shade, she paused under the first tree and listened. Nothing.

"Mr Muffet?" Was that someone moving around in the copse? 'Mr Muffet!'

Percival Muffet emerged from behind a coppiced oak, ducking under a long curved bough. He looked tired and dusty and oddly…wet.

"There you are!"

He seemed appalled to see her; rather affronting, really. "Oh, Lady Kerenza. You shouldn't have come all this way. The dam- dreadful animal has run off even further."

"Perhaps we can entice him back with these?" She proffered the bowl.

"Her. It's a female." He sighed and took the bowl. There was a definite *odour* about him. What on Earth had happened? "Perhaps. Still, we shouldn't be here. Alone, I mean."

He was right, of course. It was dreadfully *fast* of her to be in a wood with a man who wasn't a member of her family. She waved that off.

"The welfare of the monkey is more important. Besides, who will know? Let's call her name."

The man looked absolutely blank. Really, these people should *not* be in charge of *any* animal!

"She *does* have a name, doesn't she?"

Rather shamefacedly, Mr Muffet shrugged. Kerenza bit back a smile. He looked like a schoolboy who had been lectured.

"Feel free to name her yourself, my lady. If you left it to me, I'd call her the Devil's daughter."

She did laugh at that. "Oh, dear. As bad as that? Where does she come from, do you know?"

"Arabia. She's a hamadryas baboon."

A baboon.

"Not a monkey?"

They turned and walked back into the copse, side by side. "*Like* a monkey, the keeper who delivered her said. But not. Something about no tail."

"What does she eat, apart from berries?"

"*Everything.* She's like a goat. *Worse* than a goat! Grass, fruit, our gardener's precious new dahlias, beetles, the horses' hot mash, my father's Sunday roast beef—anything and everything she can get her hands on. But for Heaven's sake don't feed her underripe acorns. They have a…a deleterious effect on her digestion."

Kerenza began to laugh and then couldn't stop. "Oh, you poor things! Still, that makes it easier." She stopped to consider. "I think I shall name her Genevieve."

"*Genevieve?*"

"There was a particularly gluttonous governess we had once, Miss Genevieve Turbot."

THIS GIRL WAS TEASING him mercilessly. Percival fixed her with a stern gaze.

"She cannot possibly have been named Miss Turbot!"

She gurgled with laughter. "No. Her name was Talbot. But she ate *so much* fish that Lion christened her Turbot."

"Perhaps we should call the baboon Turbot, then."

"No! On no account. She's a beautiful animal and she deserves a beautiful name." Looking up into the tree above them, she crooned, "Don't you, Genevieve?"

Good Lord, the animal was there! How had she *done* that? It felt like magic.

"Poor Genevieve," Lady Kerenza said. "You're cold and lonely and hungry, aren't you?" She took the strawberries from him and held them out. In the same tone, she said, "If you could back away, Mr Muffet, I think I can coax her down."

Nothing loath, he moved away—but not too far. That animal had bitten one of the stable boys, and he couldn't let any harm come to Lady Kerenza.

It looked like some allegorical painting: the beautiful young woman, holding a bowl of strawberries up to a wild animal. The fruit almost glowed in the shade of the oak, and Lady Kerenza's face was like a Madonna's. Perfect.

A pang pierced his heart. Perfect, and un-touchable for one from his background. No matter how gentlemanlike he *appeared,* he wasn't gentry and never would be. Let alone nobility. He shouldn't even be gazing at her like this. He couldn't look away.

Slowly, with Lady Kerenza's warm voice luring her, the baboon came down the tree, and then jumped straight into the girl's arms, wrapping all four limbs around her and burying its dog-like face in her neck.

"There. You're all right now. Have a strawberry." She turned until she could see Percival clearly, over the top of the baboon's head. In a quiet, soothing voice, she said, "Her breath would knock a ploughman over! I shall get her some mint to chew."

He moved forwards to take the burden from her, but the baboon—Genevieve, for God's sake!—raised her head and bared her teeth, chittering nastily.

"No, no, my sweet," Kerenza said soothingly. "It's all right. Mr Muffet will just walk beside us."

"She's too heavy for you!"

"Nonsense! She's mostly fur. No heavier than a two-year-old child, although she is a little long. I'll be fine. Let's take her to the old dairy."

THE GIRL SMELT OF LEMONS. She had brought berries. She was a friend.

This was better than pissing on the-man-who-locked-her-up, although that had been funny.

The girl might take her to her troop leader, and she could go home. She clung tighter and glared at the male.

AS THEY WALKED BACK across the lawn and around the side of the house to the outbuildings behind, Percival prayed devoutly that no one would see. It wasn't just the baboon—

although bringing a wild animal to a house party was completely beyond the pale. He was dirty, dusty, his boots were scratched, he was damp and smelly, and he was sure his cravat was crumpled.

If only he could bolt! He shouldn't even *be* with Lady Kerenza. They hadn't been formally introduced. He had no idea how she'd known who he was. Then he realised—their coach would be the only one arriving without a crest on the panel. Rather downputting.

Anyone meeting them would probably think he was a servant. An upper servant, of course, in these clothes. The earl's secretary, perhaps, or a damned music teacher.

He couldn't abandon her. What an amazing girl she was! That gown, of the finest muslin, was being scratched and dirtied by the Devil's daughter, but she seemed totally unconcerned. Her hair was half fallen, her cheeks flushed, and there were patches of sweat on the back of her gown. He shouldn't notice them.

They made her feel more like a real person. Instead of a Madonna in a painting.

She led him to a small stone building half-sunken into the ground. The door was closed, but not locked, so he opened it for her and they passed in. A plain stone room with stone troughs along one side. Some wooden crates stood in one corner, with a pile of potato sacks on top.

"Papa's herd has outgrown this dairy, so he built a new one," Lady Kerenza explained over her shoulder. "Can you spread those sacks in a sink for me, please?"

Once he'd hurried to do that, she lowered the baboon into the nicely padded trough, emptying the last of the strawberries in her lap.

"Better not leave her the bowl. Mrs Lovell would have my neck if she broke it. Now, we'll need water and some blankets; this place is designed to be cold, so she'll be freezing in here without a snug bed. And some more nourishing food, too."

"How are we going to explain all this to your parents?"

Astonishingly, she giggled.

HE *WAS* FUNNY!

"As if we'll tell them anything! My word, if they knew *half* of what we all get up to!" She shook her head. "No. Definitely not. It would embarrass your father and serve no useful purpose. You can tell him once the party is over and you need to take her home. She'll be fine here until then."

Mr Muffet hadn't expected that. He blinked, and then slowly his mouth pursed in an admiring smile.

"You're a marvel!" he said. He took her hand and kissed it, with quite an air. Was he a flirt? Or even a *rake*? No, she couldn't believe that. He wasn't good-looking enough to be a rake.

Then he looked up at her over her hand, and she revised that opinion. Not *classically* handsome. But what eyes! Greyish and deep and full of charm. A small thrill went through her, which was *not right*.

Mr Muffet was not to be trifled with. It wasn't fair to him to flirt with him. He was totally unsuitable.

Which was a shame. But really: imagine being called Muffet!

THIS WAS NOT A *BAD* PLACE. It was dark and she had berries. Then a large one came, a male, with food. Good. She would stay here for a while. Perhaps the-girl-who-smelt-of-lemons would bring her troop leader, and she could go home.

CHAPTER 4

She contrived with Bryok to smuggle Mr Muffet into the house, and then confided in him about the baboon.

Bryok was solid. He grinned, but that was fair.

"Miss Melissa will know what's best for the animal," he suggested.

That was true. Melissa knew all kinds of things you wouldn't expect.

"No. We have to keep this as secret as possible. Imagine how embarrassed the Muffets would be if it got out! The Prince Regent would be furious!"

The mention of royalty sobered him. "Right you are, Miss Keri."

Was she never to be called 'my lady' by the servants? She grinned internally. Not by Bryok when she was enrolling him in a mischief, at least.

"I must get myself presentable before the rest of the guests arrive. You take the blankets and food out, and tell the kitchen Mr Muffet brought–" What *could* he have brought which wouldn't be scandalously rude? There was no animal which fell within the bounds of polite society. "Oh, don't tell them anything! Get some of Ives' old blankets from the boat locker."

"Yes, miss." He was openly teasing now. "I mean, yes, *my lady*."

"And don't you forget it, my lad!" She bit her lip to stop laughing out loud, and snuck up the servants' stairs to her room, feeling no more than ten years old and about to be scolded by her governess.

Lud, that had been fun!

Now to make herself presentable.

.　.　.

WHEN SHE ENTERED the drawing room twenty minutes later, there were both Mr Muffets, and the younger one had cleaned up nicely.

Now for the charade.

She knew his father already, since he came to the Hall often on business.

A stern and solid man, conscious of his social position and never putting himself forward in company, no matter how many times he'd visited. Full of rectitude and rules. Poor Mr Muffet.

Other guests had arrived; she knew some, but not others, so the introduction to *her* Mr Muffet was neatly sandwiched between others.

He bowed neatly, with no sign they'd already met. Reining himself in to protect her reputation. A wash of relief made her smile weak.

"Mr Percival Muffet." Her mother presented him, but her brother Lion cut in.

"Percy, Mama. Don't saddle him with Percival!"

"Not much better," Mr Muffet said, raising his eyebrows.

"Val is better," Melissa interjected. "Connotations of valour and being valiant."

He bowed to Melissa. "Thank you, Lady Melissa. That *would* be better."

Mama laughed. "Mr *Val* Muffet. Mr Muffet, Lady Kerenza."

Val. *Much* better than Percival. Sir Percival in the stories of King Arthur had always been such a prig. She hadn't realised that he and Lion were acquaintances. Mr Muffet must have gone to Harrow. Being called Endellion was a burden to her brother—no wonder he'd offered Mr Muffet a nickname. In their schooldays, Lion would probably have just called him 'Muffet'. Boys did that.

She dipped her best curtsey. "Mr Muffet."

"Lady Kerenza."

And then on to the next one, the Earl of

Merryam and his mother Phoebe, the countess. They seemed nice—the earl was only a few years older than she was, and was tall and handsome. If her mother hadn't had that rule about being too young to marry, she'd think he'd been invited as a matchmaking ploy. Which wouldn't have been bad at all. He really was very handsome. And an earl.

But, listening to the conversation, sipping tea genteelly as a young lady should, she realised that he and her mother had charitable enterprises in mind, and he had been invited, apparently, so they could plan a Poor School in Soho.

She had to stop thinking that this party was about her. Her birthday had provided the excuse for the ball, but everyone coming would be here with their own plans and priorities, and she would be the least of their concerns. Look at her sister Delmelza in her widow's weeds, pale and thin, venturing into company for the first time since her husband's death. Or Melissa sliding backwards out of the room; she'd had her limit of company and would make off to the library. Charles Goddard followed her; he was the Earl of Westholm and had some important work in the government in which he used Melissa's skill with languages quite often, although Kerenza wasn't supposed to know about that.

Yes, they were all going about their business and not thinking about her.

That was rather freeing.

"LADY BEATRICE, may I present Mr Val Muffet. Mr Muffet, Lady Beatrice Marlowe."

He bowed. Lady Beatrice was a tall brunette with an air of quiet decorum. She curtsied and smiled. Over her shoulder, he caught the countess exchanging a meaningful glance with his father.

Surely they couldn't be matchmaking?

Involuntarily, he looked for Lady Kerenza.

In company, she sat quietly and didn't put herself forward; it was as though she were a different girl altogether. Well trained, as he had been, but for a very different purpose. No doubt Lord Merryam had been invited on her behalf; these nobles liked to marry their girls off early.

The thought gave him an itch inside; an urge to move which he couldn't give in to. Lady Beatrice turned to speak with the Merryam countess, thank goodness, so he went to his father's side, by the earl. Calmly, politely, he answered Earl Trengrouse's questions about his time at Cambridge and his intentions now.

"You've gone into the business with your father, heh, Val?" Lord Trengrouse said.

Val. He *did* like that name. He cast a sceptical look at his father.

"If he'll let me, sir." He'd been helping his father over the last year or so, since he'd come down from Cambridge. The war in France had meant they were working at full capacity, to supply the Army. It was satisfying to know he'd helped his country. But lately his father had been edging him out.

"What! Why wouldn't he?"

Mr Muffet sat forward. "Now the war is over, we're cutting production for a while, and I don't need him. I've a mind to buy him an estate he can manage, my lord. No need for him to toil in the manufactory."

Lord Trengrouse laughed. "You make it sound like a salt mine! Does young men no harm to work. Mine do. Petroc's Army, of course, and Locryn manages the estate side of things, but Lion runs our shipping, Felix is a mining engineer, and Ives will handle the transport of the tin now he's finished at Oxford."

"You see, Father?"

If only Father would let him do something *useful*. He'd rather be a fully-fledged Cit who achieved something in the world than a not-quite-gentry shunned by an entire district, even if working in the manufactory office was…less than absorbing.

"It's well and good for your sons, my lord. No one's going to be calling them a Cit or a mushroom."

Lord Trengrouse laughed. "Those days are dying. More and more up-and-coming men are like you and your son. Self-made, and none the worse for that!"

Father smiled sourly. "There's not many of your mind, my lord, and well you know it."

"Nonsense!"

His father's eyes snapped. "Nonsense, is it? Then I suppose you'd be pleased if your girl over there were to take a fancy to marry my son?"

Oh no. Lord Trengrouse took in a breath, but Val forestalled him. "As if Lady Kerenza would look twice at me, Father. Or marry to disoblige her family. It's insulting to even suggest it."

Lord Trengrouse assessed him, his gaze keen. "I wouldn't say an insult, lad. You're of good stock." His gaze flicked to Lady Beatrice and back. "For the right woman, you'd be a fine catch. But Keri has her heart set on a lord with a townhouse in London. And what she wants, she usually gets. She'll probably bring home a duke!"

"He'd be a lucky man indeed," Val said. Of course she would bring home a duke.

Father had noticed that glance at Lady Beatrice and fallen silent. Why on Earth would they think he might be suitable for her?

Nodding, Lord Trengrouse laughed. "Lucky to know if he were on his head or his heels! Whoever marries Keri will be happy, but he'll never know a quiet moment."

Exactly his impression of her. Wonderful, but impossible. Doubly impossible for him.

His father launched into the story of visiting the Prince Regent's menagerie in the Tower of London and being given a baboon. The other men laughed.

"Just like Prinny!" Earl Trengrouse said. "Palming his problems off onto others."

"It's true the cages were very small and dark. And full," Val said.

When they'd gone to collect the Devil's daughter, he'd been appalled at the crowded, smelly cages and lack of light for the poor animals.

Surely there were better ways to keep them? He'd written to Sir Anthony, the Head of the Menagerie, to suggest some changes and to offer his help, but had heard nothing back.

Of course, most humans didn't have reasonable living conditions. He said as much.

Earl Trengrouse agreed, and the conversation became about politics in general and how much still needed to be done to stamp out slavery. His father listened, brows twitched together as though he disapproved of Val having any opinions at all. Well, he could lump it. *He wanted me to be a gentleman? This is what a gentleman does. Concerns himself with things greater than the factory floor.*

ON THE WAY TO dress for dinner, his father paused outside Val's door and took him by the lapel.

"That Lady Beatrice...the countess tells me her family has fallen on hard times. Entailed estate went to a cousin after the father and brother were both killed in a carriage accident, and the cousin isn't providing for her. No dowry to speak of."

Ah. *That's* why he might be suitable for her. Because she was poor, and he was rich; or his father was. All this talk of an estate made more sense. A lady wouldn't want her husband to be in trade. He could feel a comfortable but essentially meaningless life being wrapped around him like a smothering blanket.

"Even so, Father. She doesn't strike me as someone who'd settle for second best."

"If the countess and the earl think you're good enough for her, then you are!"

For such a normally hard-headed man, Father put far too much stock in what the nobility thought.

"Let's wait until *she* decides that, shall we?"

"Hmph!"

Father went into his room. For a moment, Val stayed motionless. He had no idea, *none,* what he could do to get out of all this.

Perhaps he shouldn't try. Lady Beatrice would be a good wife, he was sure, and she was certainly beautiful. A calm, quiet, poised beauty. He put away an image of a dishevelled, luscious Kerenza carrying the baboon out of the copse.

Not for him. Not ever.

SHE WAS COLD. The-girl-who-smelt-of-lemons, the one who had called her by a name that was wrong, had gone long ago, and the-male-with-food didn't stay.

The food was good, but it was gone.

It was cold. She looked up. Yes, this place was like the-place-that-smelt-of-horses where they had locked her up. The roof was just straw, tied together with more straw that she could easily chew through.

She threw off the sacks and climbed up the rough wall easily. It was warmer up here, and it would be even warmer outside.

She put her teeth to the straw and bit.

CHAPTER 5

After breakfast the next day, Bryok caught Kerenza as she moved from the table.

"Miss Keri…the…that package you asked me to look after for you has…been moved."

She froze.

"A problem, Kerenza?" her mother asked.

"No, no. I just forgot to tell Bryok that I'd taken a parcel up to my room." She gazed meaningfully at him, and he nodded slightly.

Her mother went out. "Where has it gone?" Keri whispered fiercely.

"Honest to God, Miss Keri, I don't know.

I went to feed it this morning, and it was gone. There was a hole in the thatch."

The devil's daughter was cunning. Those clever hands, and those clever eyes and teeth.

"All right. I'll deal with it," she said. Bryok looked relieved, and began to gather the dishes from the table.

This was the day of the ball. They *had* to find that animal *now*! Before the guests began arriving.

Where would it have gone?

There was always food in the stables, if you could get the lids of the oat bins open, and she had no doubt Genevieve could.

She passed Ives and Val in the passageway to the kitchen. Ives was talking about going fishing in his smack. She glared meaningfully at Val.

"But Mr Muffet said he wanted to see the stables this morning, Ives. *Didn't you?*"

At least he was quick-witted. "Yes, I did indeed. Sorry, Trengrouse."

"Day after tomorrow, then. I'll wake you

early." Tomorrow they would all sleep in after the very late hours of the ball.

"Do that," Val said. Ives went off with a wave of his hand and she took Val's arm in a firm grip, leading him down the passageway. "It got out, didn't it? This is going to ruin Papa and me."

"Nonsense. We'll find it quickly enough. The closest place to the old dairy with food is the stables. Let's check there first."

WHEN THEY GOT to the stables, he had time for only a brief glance. They weren't alone.

Lady Beatrice moved forward out of the dimness, smiling calmly.

"Mr Muffet! Have you come to ride?"

"No, no," he stuttered. "Lady Kerenza was showing me, um–"

"I wanted to show him Blackfoot's new colt," Kerenza cut in. A life-saver.

Petroc Trengrouse was behind her. It looked like he was about to mount a grey horse. Good for him. Petroc, although they'd been friends as children, made Val feel like—well, like not much of a man. A soldier, wounded at Waterloo, and still valiantly carrying on his normal life. Next to him, Val didn't make much of a show.

Beatrice led them out, while he tried to make normal conversation with both of them. It was only a short walk to the paddock, where a young colt raced across the grass.

"Look!" Kerenza cried. "Isn't he adorable?"

He was a fine animal. The three of them leant on the fence and watched. How soon could they get away? Impatience burned in him, but he couldn't be rude.

"Nice conformation," Beatrice said. "What's his breeding?"

"By Hartigan out of Blackfoot." The dam, a bay, was nearby. "Blackfoot traces back to the Godolphin Barb, and Hartigan's from the Smetanka line."

He had no idea what any of that meant.

Something important, by the impressed look on Lady Beatrice's face.

"How on Earth did your father achieve that?" she asked.

"Oh, you know Father. Favours here, favours there, and things happen. He bought a mare in foal from them, and luckily it was a colt."

His hand, without him wishing it, tapped on the fence.

"We're boring Mr Muffet," Lady Beatrice said. "Not everyone is horse-mad."

"They are in *this* family." Kerenza wrinkled her nose. "I like them when they're tiny, but I do get tired of all the breeding rigmarole."

He had to contribute to this conversation or they'd think he was a know-nothing.

"You like to ride, though, Lady Kerenza," he said.

"Well, of course!"

Of course. He'd been put on a horse for the first time not far from here, on an old, placid mare which had taught all the Trengrouses to ride. He'd been sore for days afterwards, but it had made him determined to learn how to ride properly, and he had, once he was out of school. But it was different when you'd been born to it. Over to the right, Petroc was cantering the grey. Even with one leg, he had a better seat than Val.

He kept one ear cocked for a disturbance in the stables—or anywhere else.

"Have you known the Trengrouses long, Mr Muffet?"

Smile, man. Act natural. "Most of my life, Lady Beatrice. Our fathers have been in business together for quite some time, and I used to come with him when he visited. Until I went to school."

Her gaze was very slightly pitying, as if she understood how out of place he felt. "Now you have the fun of getting to know them all as adults," she suggested.

Oh yes. Such fun. Although, Kerenza… she'd been barely out of baby clothes, he reckoned, when he'd first visited and, like the rest of the boys, he'd paid the babies no mind. "Indeed. Enough about the Trengrouses! Tell me about yourself, Lady Beatrice. Are you looking forward to the ball?"

They spoke about the festivities for a while, both watching the colt.

Kerenza tripped back to them, a smile on her face. "Come on, you two! Stop cozing! It's time to decorate the ballroom." She tucked her hand in his arm, and Lady Beatrice did the same on the other side.

Back to the house? But–

"Oh, how silly of me!" Kerenza exclaimed. "I must have dropped my handkerchief in the stables."

"I'll go and get it." He relinquished their arms, bowed, and sped off to the stables. Kerenza was a genius, God bless her.

THE-MAN-WHO-LOCKED-HER-UP was looking in the horse place. Heheheh.

She wasn't stupid enough to go near there.

She watched him from the trees at the

edge of the green space. He could look all day and he would never find her.

But the-girl-who-smelt-of-lemons was going away.

She sighed. No berries now. Maybe she could find other fruit. Or even roots.

IT WAS hard to concentrate on talking to Beatrice on the walk back to the house; Keri couldn't help hoping that Val—she must think of him as Mr Muffet!—had found Genevieve safe and sound.

Once they were inside the ballroom, they were immediately swept up in the general tasks of selecting and arranging blooms in vases. Melissa had set up a sample vase for them all to copy. Beatrice was particularly good at it, although she kept getting distracted by Petroc. It was nice that they were becoming friends. Petroc could use a friend right now.

A few minutes later, Val came in. Their eyes met and he shook his head just a little.

Bother! Where else could she have gone? Back to the oak copse, perhaps?

Then Petroc swung over to her on his crutches, and held something out. Oh, her birthday present!

"Happy Birthday, Keri." She put her hand out with glee, but it was papers instead of a present. She opened the packet with intense curiosity. What on Earth could this be?

Stunned, she gazed at the writing. Shares in the Trengrouse tin mine. Shares in the Trengrouse shipping company. The *boys* had all got shares when they turned fifteen. None of the girls did.

"But-these are shares." Astonished, everyone crowded around.

"Yes," he said. "Held in trust for you. Mama and Lady Marlowe are your trustees. It should provide you with a little independent income."

Independent? *Income* of her very own? Warmth exploded through her, and she was dizzy at the thought. Women *never* had income of their own!

"Th-thank you."

Demelza and Melissa were ranked at her back.

"Why Kerenza?" Demelza asked, in a voice like ice. Quite right. It wasn't fair that she should have shares and not the other two. Petroc blanched but rallied.

"I thought I'd talk to the others—Locryn and the others—and see if we couldn't find parcels of shares for you and Melissa as well," he said. "It's not good for a woman to be completely dependent on her husband. Or on getting a husband."

His gaze flicked to Beatrice, who stood up from her table. Val was staring at him as though he was mad.

"It certainly isn't," Elestryn said. "That was well thought of."

"You'll set a trend," Val said. "I hope my sisters don't hear about this—it might bankrupt us!" That was disappointing. She'd rather thought he'd be more progressive.

Petroc chuckled. "Do you have many?"

"Six!" Val said in tones of despair.

Everyone laughed. Six sisters. No wonder he was hesitant to split up the company. They only had the one source of income, after all.

Now *she* had an independent income. It wouldn't be a lot. But it meant…it meant she could make her own choices. For the very first time, she realised that she might not need to marry, if she couldn't find a man she liked.

Or she could marry *whomever* she liked. Even if Papa refused to hand over her dowry, she wouldn't come to a marriage penniless.

She shook herself out of that thought and turned to Mr Muffet. "Come with me to get some more greenery from the gardener," she said.

They *had* to find that animal before the ball.

The children were in the orchard, and joined in with the search enthusiastically.

"A monkey!" they shouted. "Huzzah!"

"A baboon," she said. Demelza's twin girls were giggling at the thought, which was lovely to see; they'd lost their father only a month ago.

She made searching for the animal a game, and they all joined in with verve until called back by the twins' governess for afternoon tea.

SHE LIKED THIS GAME.

She and the two small ones who smelled alike found each other early, but they pretended not to see her. After that, she followed them silently, and would grin at them from behind a bush until they fell over laughing.

It was almost like having a troop again.

But she couldn't come out and play with the others, because the-man-who-locked-her-up was there.

ALTHOUGH SHE AND Mr Muffet continued searching after the children went inside, they found no sign of Genevieve.

"I have to go back," Kerenza said at last,

slumping on a seat in the summerhouse. "Mama wants me to rest this afternoon so I'm in good looks tonight."

"No danger you won't be," Val muttered, and she smiled to herself. He cleared his throat and stood up straight. "Perhaps I can-perhaps we could…would you save me a dance, perhaps?"

He was so sweet!

"Of course." And here was an opportunity to make sure she was with someone for supper whom she knew she could talk to. So the short break would be a real rest from the tensions of the night. "The supper dance!" she declared.

He looked startled, but pleased. "I'll look forward to it." Putting out a hand, he pulled her to her feet. "Let's get you back to your Mama. Genevieve has probably found an apple tree full of fruit."

"We checked the orchard," she said absently, brushing a twig from her gown. Where had she picked that up? "But she might have found a single tree somewhere.

The boys used to bury their apple cores, so there are apple trees all through the woods."

His face showed dismay at the thought of tramping through all of the woodland on the estate, and she laughed as he took his arm.

"Don't worry. After the ball we can muster the entire staff to help look for her."

After the ball. She smiled up at him with simple happiness, and saw his expression change to something she'd never seen in a man's eyes before.

She wasn't sure quite what it was, but it was thrilling.

CHAPTER 6

"$\mathcal{A}$ word in your ear, lad." His father took hold of his lapel and Val had to stop impatiently.

His bedroom door was only steps away— his valet Shepherd awaited. After Keri had gone up, he'd looked for another hour or so, and if he didn't get changed he'd be late for dinner.

"Yes, Pa?"

"Father! I've told you–"

"Father." Val sighed. He remembered the holidays spent following his father around the factory floor, before all this nonsense about being a gentleman had started. "Pa" had been good enough then; but not now.

"In here." His father nodded to Val's room, and they went inside. Shepherd, his valet, took in the situation immediately and made himself scarce. Below their feet, the sound of the ballroom being prepared came up: clink of china and cutlery, the swish of a broom, a fiddler tuning up.

"What's the matter, *Father*?"

"This Lady Beatrice. I want to see you make an effort tonight."

Val closed his eyes briefly. There was no arguing with the man. The determination and drive which had led him to a manufacturing fortune wouldn't be denied. His father ploughed on.

"She's a real lady, that one. Never turns a hair. And pretty, too."

Pretty? Beautiful, rather, but cool.

"I doubt she'd–"

"Her own cousin threw her out of her home!" Pa's voice was full of condemnation, and rightly so. What a bounder the man must be. "She and her mother have barely enough to put food on the table. You'd be *rescuing* her!"

A flicker of uncertainty wormed into his brain. Really? That bad? She didn't *look* poor.

His father was a shrewd negotiator, and he backed off now. "Well, well. Just a word in your ear. Get to know her, that's all I ask. It would open doors for you, lad."

And for you, Val thought, but knew he was being petty.

"And for your sisters." Pa gave him a stern look. "Rose and Janet are settled nicely, but the younger ones could look higher, with a lady for their sister-in-law."

They could. Whether that would make them any happier than his older sisters, both glowing with content in their marriages to Cits, was another question.

"I'll bear that in mind," he said.

"Good lad!" A clap on the shoulder, and the old man was out the door. Shepherd slid in the next moment.

"I've drawn a bath for you in the dressing room, sir," he said.

Abruptly aware that he smelt of stables and mud, Val nodded.

He'd have to dance with the woman anyway, out of normal politeness. Maybe a waltz. That should placate his father.

But not the supper dance.

SHE WAS BORED.

And hungry.

The small ones had gone away. The sun was going down.

She couldn't remember last time she'd spent a night outside.

An old, half-forgotten part of her knew it was dangerous to be out in the night without her troop.

She would go back to the cold place and sleep once it grew dark.

It wasn't dark *yet*.

CHAPTER 7

Her mother sighed. "You look so grown up."

"I *am* grown up!" Kerenza said, twirling in front of the mirror, the white satin of her dress shimmering as she moved. Mama had allowed her to have blue ribbons at her bodice and on the sleeves, and it made all the difference. Wait until her best friend Katie saw her!

Her parents had given her a pearl necklace, Locryn pearl earrings, Lion an ivory fan, Melissa and Ives a pearl-studded hair comb, Demelza a pale blue Paisley shawl,

Felix a pearl bracelet, and Petroc, of course, had given her the parcel of shares in the mine!

It was quite revolutionary of Petroc; perhaps recuperating by the sea with Mama's friend, the dowager Countess of Mannering and Lady Beatrice (known to be in straitened circumstances), had shown him how precarious many women's lives were.

She was perfectly dressed, and she was *rich*! This was already a night to remember.

"Come, grown-up daughter," Mama said, laughing at her. "We must be on time to greet our guests."

How would Mr Muffet react when he saw her dressed like this?

Keri tossed her head at the thought and made for the door. Really, she shouldn't care what he thought!

Yet, when his eyes widened and he coloured slightly as she came down the staircase, a curl of satisfaction unfurled below her heart.

·   ·   ·

THE SUN WAS VERY low in the sky. Time to go inside. But she smelled fruit. Apples. She knew apples. The head of her troop gave her apples. Perhaps he was at the apple place.

Jumping down from the cold building, she ran, enjoying the grass under her feet and the wind in her face.

Apples!

THE SMALL PEOPLE were in the apple trees. She froze. But the-man-who-locked-her-up wasn't there.

"Look!" a small one said. "The monkey!"

She knew that word. People who said that word often gave her food, so she loped over to the small one and squatted, waiting.

Sure enough, the small one offered her an apple.

Yes. This was the way the world was supposed to work. People looked at her, and gave her food.

The apple was good.

The other small ones came, patting her

and saying things she didn't listen to. The ones who smelled alike gave her another apple.

One of those took her hand.

"Come with me," it said. She knew those words. There was usually more food if she obeyed.

The small ones walked with her towards the stone mountain place. She wasn't sure, but when she stopped, the biggest of the troop picked her up, and she clung to him—he smelled like a male—because it was good to be part of a troop again.

The smaller ones all patted her and she relaxed. Food and company. The small ones might take her to her troop leader.

"Shhh!" one said. "You know we're not supposed to be out here!"

They were all quiet. Predators about? She knew how to be quiet; her mother had taught her, a long time ago.

Thinking about her mother made her sad, so she clung to the male and buried her face in his shoulder.

He smelled like home, of straw and apple and other animals, and his hands were gentle. She wouldn't piss on this one.

AT DINNER, Keri was seated between Lord Merryam and Denzell Kelynack, an old friend and brother to her best friend. It was Katie's first ball too. She sat opposite, next to Mr Muffet, with Lady Beatrice on his other side.

Katie was in fine form, apparently, going by Val's smiles. Mr *Muffet's* smiles. It was quite irregular of her to think of him as Val and she had to stop, or she might say his name in an unguarded moment, and what a scandal that would be!

The Trengrouse dining room was huge, of course—it had to be. Even during an informal dinner, they sat sixteen down, just with family. Tonight there was forty, and after dinner the room would be turned into the supper room. It was on the ground floor because her grandfather had insisted he pre-

ferred his food hot, not tepid because servants had to climb innumerable stairs to get
it to the old dining room.

In London, they had dumbwaiters to
send the food directly up from the kitchen to
the diners. She lost herself for a moment in a
happy dream of their London townhouse
and how wonderful her Season would be.

Tonight would be wonderful too, once
the ball started.

Unlike at many estates, the ballroom at
Trengrouse Hall was also on the ground
floor, in the old north wing, with pairs of
doors which opened onto the terrace and
gardens. It was reached through a gallery
which led from the dining room to the old
main entrance in the north wing. Guests for
the ball would enter through there, rather
than coming all the way through the house.

"Are you interested in charity work, Lady
Kerenza?" Lord Merryam asked.

"Good Lord no!" The words slipped out,
and she bit her lip. "I mean, I'm involved on
the estate, of course, making sure the tenants

are well cared for. And our servants. But I haven't been roped-asked to join in any of Mama's projects." It would be more interesting if the charity projects were aimed at animals; so many horses and ponies were ill-treated.

"I suppose," he said slowly, "down here you don't see much of the terrible poverty we see in London."

"There's poverty everywhere," Katie's brother Den said, right across her, as if they were in a family dinner. "But it's easier to notice in the country; and easier to do something about it. More of a family-by-family affair, not village-by-village."

"Suburb-by-suburb, in London." He caught sight of her face, and paused. "Not suitable discussion for a dinner party, Lady Kerenza?"

"It is rather dispiriting," she admitted. "Let's talk about something less...challenging."

Lord Merryam laughed. "What did you have in mind?"

"Ask her about her upcoming Season," Den advised. "It's all the girls are talking about. Katie's the same."

Katie seemed like her attention was on Mr Muffet, but that was just her being polite. She wasn't the kind of girl who would even *think* about marrying to disoblige her family. Her mother was too overbearing for that. Beatrice Marlowe, though…she was in reduced circumstances. A well-heeled Cit might not be out of the question for her. And she was smiling at Val.

"I am looking forward to it," she admitted, forcing herself to look away. "It's only natural. Katie and I will have so much fun, coming out together!"

They talked about when they would all remove to London for the Season, and some of the upcoming events. They would go up in October, for the Little Season, Mama said, "so you can find your footing before the world and his wife arrives." Now that the war with Napoleon was over, the capital would be full of young men, free to enjoy their lives. Apart from those who, like Petroc, had come home maimed.

No, she wouldn't think about sad things tonight!

"My Mama will no doubt be sending you invitations for her rout. She always has it early in the Season, before Easter," Lord Merryam said.

"How jolly!"

Yes. She and Katie would go to London and flirt with earls and dukes and mar-quesses, and dance all night and dress in marvellous frocks and be a Success! How nice it would be to already know some people there. She smiled at Lord Merryam with real warmth.

SHE WAS SMILING at that earl. Val stopped himself from scowling and listened to Miss Kelynack. She was a Miss, because her brother was only a baronet. Thank god he'd memorised all the proper titles, honorary and substantive, from Debrett's.

Like Kerenza being Lady Kerenza but her brothers being merely Honourables, not Lords. Daughters of earls got honorary titles, but the sons didn't. None of this etiquette made any sense, and it was clearly designed to trip up outsiders, to show who belonged and who didn't.

Damn it, he was determined it wouldn't trip *him* up.

"Will you be in London for the Season, Mr Muffet?" Miss Kelynack asked.

"That will depend on whether my father needs me in the business," he said. Show them he wasn't ashamed of where he came from, that was the ticket.

"Of course." She nodded, and then the course was changed and she turned, most correctly, to the other side to speak with Ives Trengrouse. It was his turn to talk to Lady Beatrice.

They spoke easily together of their journeys to Cornwall. She and her mother had moved there eighteen months ago; presumably that was after her father and brother's deaths, although she didn't mention that. For him, it had been a long trip from the Midlands. If only he'd known that dashed baboon was on board!

He lost track of what she was saying, and she smiled at him quizzically. "Wool-gathering, Mr Muffet?"

"I'm so sorry, Lady Beatrice. I must be more tired than I realised."

She was so poised, it was like having dinner with a model of A Lady. "A long journey will have that effect. The salmon is good, isn't it?"

Ah yes. Let's talk about the food. The last resort of the dinner table. He couldn't help himself; he laughed.

"We can find something better to discuss than the salmon, my lady. Tell me about your home in Swain Cove. Petroc informs me that he is staying there to recuperate from the-from his wound."

Her smile this time was genuine. "Semper House? Oh, there's not much to tell…"

But the telling took them through to the next course, which was all he asked.

THE SMALL ONES wandered around for a while, until the sun was almost down. They stopped and played; she ate some flowers and they laughed.

Then, as they went towards a door in the stone mountain, she saw the-girl-who-smelt-of-lemons through a window, and jumped out of the small male's arms to find her.

She scampered to the window and jumped up on its surrounds. The girl saw her and looked surprised.

That was good. Last time, the girl had brought berries.

She would have waited, but the small male grabbed her and ran away, the other small ones scolding her.

She'd been bad. She knew she wasn't supposed to run away.

But how else would she find the berries?

· · ·

KERI WAS FACING the big bay window in the middle of the dining room wall, which looked out onto the courtyard. Outside the window, one of the gardeners was fixing flaming torches either side of the doors from the north foyer, in case guests wanted to cool off in the formal gardens during the dancing. Her excitement fizzed in her veins. It was almost time!

The footmen came forward to clear the last of the dishes, and her mother sent a glance around the table, collecting the attention of the ladies. They would rise, and then they'd all move, in order of precedence, to the north wing.

A flash of something—was that eyes?—came from outside the window. Keri faltered as she rose. Yes! A dog-like face peered in. Genevieve! Oh, the poor thing looked so piteous. She must be hungry.

Keri looked for Val, but he was talking to Katie. Bryok was behind her mother, pulling her chair out of her way. No use. Tony Merryam offered her his arm. Although she was one of the lowest in true precedence here, since it was *her* ball, he would take her in after her mama and papa.

She smiled up at him as she'd been trained to do and took his arm. As they passed Bryok, she tilted her chin towards the window. He followed her gaze, and his eyes sharpened. He nodded at her once, and she relaxed.

That was sorted. Time to enjoy herself!

CHAPTER 8

He didn't want to encourage his father's fantasy, but he had no choice but to ask Lady Beatrice to dance. It would have been abominably rude not to.

Before that, it was his duty to lead Miss Kelynack onto the floor, since he had been her dinner partner.

He danced next with Lady Melissa, as his host's daughter, a country dance. Fortunately, Lady Melissa didn't expect him to make conversation—in fact, she said so right at the beginning of the set.

"It's ridiculous to try to converse as one moves through the figures," she said. "Don't feel you have to try."

He'd bowed to conceal a laugh. She was an Original, that was for sure. He could imagine her as one of those imperious old ladies who said whatever they thought whenever they liked, and expected everyone to jump to it.

He returned Lady Melissa to the side next to Lady Beatrice, and bowed to both. They went through the pleasantries and she agreed to dance with him. Far too much of a lady to refuse, no matter what she actually thought.

A waltz. Much easier than a cotillion, but odd to hold a young woman so close. They moved amicably in silence, and he began to enjoy himself. She was a calm, quiet woman.

He was aware, out of the corner of his eye, of Keri dancing with the man who'd sat next to her at dinner. Denzell Kelynack, whom he vaguely remembered from his childhood visits. A crony of Petroc's. She looked flushed and happy. There was nothing in that to send a stab into his gut.

"You haven't asked Kerenza to dance," she said. He started and lost his footing. Why would she bring Keri up? They paused for a moment, and then resumed the dance.

"She's promised me the supper dance," he said. "And I shall insist that she honours her promise." He tried to make it a joke, but it came out serious. Lady Beatrice's gaze flicked over her face, and then she deliberately looked out, across his shoulder.

"Earl Trengrouse intends to make advantageous marriages for his children," she said.

She was warning him off. Had the countess asked her to do so? "You mean Lady Kerenza will never marry a Cit."

"Any more than one of the Trengrouse men will marry a dowerless girl like me."

He'd go bail she was talking about Petroc. He'd seen the look in her eyes when she saw him.

"A man such as the captain," he said. That

was unkind, and she flushed, but *she* had started this conversation, and it was better to be frank.

The music ended and they paused, hand still in hand.

"Perhaps you're right. My father thinks so, too." He smiled bitterly. "A pact, then, Lady Beatrice. Better to settle for each other than live alone."

She smiled wryly.

"I think you'll have more choices than I will."

He bowed over her hand and released it. "You would be my first choice in that circumstance. Never doubt it."

Beatrice curtseyed. "I think you would be mine, too, Mr Muffet." Well, that was something, he supposed. He was acceptable to *one* titled young lady.

The other titled young lady was unaccountably missing from the dance floor. His heart skipped in fear. Had something happened? Genevieve…

He returned Lady Beatrice to her mother

and bowed. What a waste of time this etiquette was!

As quickly as he could, he made his way to the terrace doors, where he had last seen Keri.

CHAPTER 9

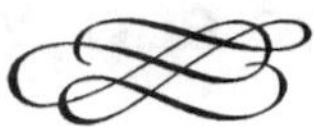

The small ones lived right at the top of the stone mountain, in a room with bars on the windows. Just like home, although the bars were set further apart.

They tucked her in a blanket under a bed. Good. Safe.

Food?

Yes. More apples and something sweet and crumbly. Biscuit! She liked biscuits.

She sighed happily and went to sleep.

When she woke, there were food smells. She peeked out from under the blanket, but the alike two quickly pushed her back. Two larger ones were there, strangers, but one fe-male smelled like the alike two's mother.

There was talking. Boring. Finally the largest one, the male, left, and the mother cuddled the alike two and went away.

Food!

She slid out from under the bed and found it. Sweet things everywhere! Good smells, good tastes. A yellow one which was the best thing she'd ever tasted. She ate fast, in case the larger ones came back. The small ones laughed and laughed to see her eat, and she grinned at them.

But then the door opened and someone shrieked. The small ones cried out, "No, Miss Lamb!"

She leapt for the window and squeezed between the bars. It was easy to climb the stone mountain up to the top.

Warm night, full moon. She stayed for a little while, enjoying the taste of sweetness and the soft wind.

Voices came up from below.

People, walking in the garden. Large ones

looked small from here. She would find the girl-who-smelled-of-lemons and get more sweet things. Or berries.

This was a good night. She liked being free. If only her troop were here with her! What fun they'd have.

BRYOK HAD MANAGED to tell her that no trace of Genevieve had been found. And then Den Kelynack asked her to dance—what a waste of a waltz! But she couldn't say no. The bonds of good manners were tight and un-forgiving.

Just as well she'd known Den since she was tiny.

"I thought I'd take the children up some treats," Denzell said in the middle of the dance, just as she was distracted by the sight of Val Muffet dancing with Beatrice Marlowe. They were talking seriously. What did they have to discuss that was so important?

She almost missed Den's question.

"Help me get a plate or two from the kitchen?"

Yes. Yes, of course. That was a good way to lure Genevieve back, too.

"Of course, Den!" She smiled up at him. "That's a lovely idea. And some for Demelza too. She's probably in the nursery with them."

Poor Demelza! Banished to the nursery by the mourning rites. It was positively medieval. Although possibly she wouldn't want to socialise anyway. Her marriage with John had been a love match.

Den's mouth tucked in on itself at Demelza's name. Keri had a vague memory of the two of them acting like April and May around each other, but that would have been a decade ago. Did he still carry a *tendre*?

Not a wonderful time to press his suit if he did, but he was no fool. He wouldn't push too hard.

After the dance ended, she managed to not look around to see what *Mr Muffet* and Beatrice were doing. She led Den back to the dining room and organised a tray for him and a plate of custard tarts for herself. Both for the children, as far as the staff was concerned.

It wasn't easy to slide unnoticed out the doors to the terrace, but she was sure the noise and activity in the central courtyard, where various couples were strolling, would send the baboon looking for sanctuary.

She went into the garden, down towards the summer house, calling gently: "Genevieve! Genevieve!"

Yes! The-girl-who-smelt-of-lemons was there, calling out the wrong name. With food!

She swiftly clambered down the mountain and scurried across the grass and gravel to her.

"Genevieve! Thank goodness!"

This was *good* food. Like the yellow things she'd eaten before. The girl gave them to her one by one, leading her towards the cold place.

No.

Grabbing the last two bits of food, Genevieve ran.

The girl ran after her.

Someone ran after the girl.

Where to go?

Up!

She stuffed the food into her mouth and jumped towards the shadowy outline of the nearest tree. But the tree was sharp and the leaves cut her. It wasn't a tree! It was metal, with harsh edges.

She fell, bleeding.

"Oh, no!" Kerenza hurried forward. Genevieve had leaped to the new iron gazebo and fallen.

Behind her, a man's steps. She whirled in surprise. Val. Thank goodness.

"She's hurt herself!"

"Let me see."

He knelt by Genevieve, who was whimpering. There was blood on her coat. She must have cut herself on the spikes along the top of the gazebo. The poor darling!

Keri hesitated. If she got blood on her ball gown… unthinkable. But the poor thing had to be cared for. She took a step forward.

"Don't worry." Val whipped off his cravat and wound it carefully around the wound on Genevieve's shoulder and arm. "It's not too bad."

He was so gentle. So *kind*. A sudden vivid memory of her grandmother saying, "Be sure to marry a man who is kind to children and animals," popped into her head.

So kind. His hands soft and precise, his face in the dim light serious and concentrating. He hadn't worried for a moment about how odd he'd look without his cravat. He'd just done what was right.

Something shifted inside her; warmth and exhilaration overwhelmed her so much, she wanted to cry. There was such deep *niceness* in him! Right down to his core.

What nobleman would act like this? None that she knew. Even Tony Merryam, so concerned with charity work, would have simply called a servant to deal with Genevieve.

Genevieve sighed and leaned against Val.

"I'll take her up to my room," he said. "My valet can watch her until after the ball is over." He grinned up at her, and her heart jumped. "And no doubt will insist on giving me a new cravat."

"Make sure you're back for the supper dance." It was all she could say, but perhaps her face showed what she was feeling, because he stood up, Genevieve in his arms, and touched her cheek gently.

"Nothing would make me miss that. Nothing."

The-man-who-locked-her-up had kind hands. Odd.

Perhaps *he* would take her to her troop leader.

He put her in a small room and told another man to look after her.

She had had enough adventures for today.

She was tired now, in pain, and sad. If her troop were here, they would hold her and comfort her and groom her, and she would know all things were good. But they weren't here. She didn't know where they were.

She thought she was safe, but she wasn't *whole* without them. She was like a single leaf on a bare tree. So alone.

She curled up on the blanket on the floor where the-man-with-kind-hands had put her.

Perhaps there would be food when she woke up.

CHAPTER 10

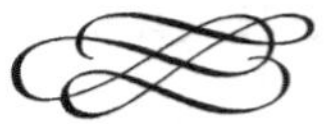

$\mathcal{I}$n her imaginings of her London Season, Keri had often envisioned the perfect supper dance.

It would be with a nobleman. An earl, at least. He would be tall and handsome. Blond with green eyes. Urbane, and witty, but struck to the heart by her beauty and charm. Her friends would look on enviously. Her family approvingly.

Here she was, with her first supper dance at a real ball…

Val Muffet was a Cit. It wasn't a kind word, perhaps, but it was just. He wasn't that tall—only an inch more than she was. He wasn't handsome. His hair was an undistinguished brown, and his eyes were grey. Ives said he had a face like a pug, and that wasn't *untrue*. He wasn't urbane. He wasn't witty.

But…his eyes, those lovely grey eyes, did gaze at her with genuine, deep affection.

And when she put her hand in his for the waltz, a thrill ran straight through her. Right down to her toes. A thing she'd never felt before.

She smiled up at him and he smiled back as they began to dance.

This was the perfect supper dance, far better than any in her imagination.

She was smiling at him as though she meant it. Val tightened his hold on Keri's waist, and she curved towards him. They danced.

Of all the skills he'd had to learn to be a "gentleman", dancing was the easiest, especially the waltz, when the music hummed through his veins and lent his feet wings.

Waltzing with Keri was like dancing on a cloud.

What a fool he was! Falling in love with her was the stupidest thing he could do, but how could he help it? It wasn't her beauty, although his whole body reacted to that.

It was her *kindness*. To him, to her nieces and nephews, to that bloody animal…

He hoped Genevieve would be all right.

Keri had a soul that glowed with goodness. He'd never be worthy of her.

He would just treasure this brief moment of being with her, and forget the future.

Over supper, the exhilaration continued. Her friend Katie had left with a megrim, but there were other friends to join them at the table, and they all treated him with a laughing disrespect which was the height of acceptance.

Keri laughed with them, and allowed her gloved hand to rest on the table so that their little fingers touched. The warmth from her hand travelled through every nerve. He shifted his leg so that their feet touched, and she didn't move away.

He was a fool. They were both fools. There was no chance her father would ever allow it.

Could this delightful, sparkling woman ever be happy as the wife of a factory owner?

No.

No point even thinking it.

Even if he followed his father's wishes, and became a gentleman farmer, the life would be so much below her that she would inevitably be unhappy.

He just couldn't move his hand away from hers.

One night. He'd just take this one night, and then let her go to London to find her duke.

A PERFECT NIGHT. Keri sighed with happiness as her maid Maryann helped her out of her ball gown while Melissa read one of her never-ending Greek books.

A tap on the door, and her mother entered. Maryann curtsied and went to help Melissa out of her dress, since she did for them both. Keri would have a maid of her own when they went to London…

"Well, daughter?" Her mother tilted her head in a question.

"Oh, what a wonderful ball, Mama! Thank you."

"Yes." Mama sat on the bed and patted the comforter so Keri would sit down beside her. "My dear…I could not help but notice that you were absent from the ballroom at one time. And so was Mr Muffet."

Keri felt the blush sweep up her chest and face. "Oh, Mama, no! It wasn't anything… anything unseemly."

"I don't care what it was, Kerenza." Mama was so rarely stern that when she was, it was shattering. Keri's stomach clenched in knots. "You are being unkind to Mr Muffet."

"Oh, no, honestly, Mama!"

Her mother held up a hand. "You are being unkind by being *too* kind." Taking a long breath, Mama let it out in a sigh. "I didn't want your father to invite them. It's not fair to a young man in his position to give him a taste for Society, when there is no chance he'd ever be received. And it was charming of you to give him the supper dance, but my dear, it wasn't kind."

Oh. She had somehow assumed that if the Muffets were received at the Hall, they would be received everywhere, but of course, that had been silly of her.

"He's a very nice young man, and I'm glad you were inclined to be nice to him. However, you're unlikely to ever see him again, once they leave, and it would be *cruel*, Kerenza, to make him believe otherwise. I don't know one hostess in London who would send him a card of invitation." She paused for emphasis. "Not one.

The words thudded into Kerenza. What had she been thinking? She knew all this. Of course she knew it! It was the way of her world. A Cit, no matter how well educated or well mannered, was beyond the pale. An impoverished lord might wed an heiress with roots in Trade, but no lady of quality would do the equivalent.

It would be social ruin.

Her mother was regarding her with pleased satisfaction. "I knew I had only to drop a word in your ear," she said. "After all, it's not as though you have a *tendre* for the young man. Not likely, with a face like that!" She laughed, but not unkindly.

How *could* she! Keri forced herself to smile, and kept it up after her mother left the room, taking Maryann with her to attend to one of the guests. She wandered over to the window and looked out at the setting moon.

"Imagine," Melissa said, studying her intently, "imagine never having to go to another Society party because one's husband was ineligible. That would be wonderful."

Keri blinked. She'd always known that Melissa didn't enjoy parties or balls the way the rest of them did, but to prefer *never* to go to one again?

She plumped herself back down on the

bed, suddenly exhausted. "But I *like* parties! I enjoy dancing and seeing people I like, and, and having *fun!*"

"Then you'd better not marry Mr Muffet." Melissa's calm good sense was devastating.

All her pleasure in that wonderful waltz disappeared.

How could she have forgotten who she was, and who he was, and remembered only that he was kind, and good, and, and, *wonderful?*

She knew better. Had been taught better. "Be kind to your inferiors, but keep a proper distance," her first governess had told her, more than once. She had kept no distance at all from Mr Muffet. No wonder Mama had warned her off.

And Mama was *right*. It wasn't fair to Val, when there was no chance at all that Papa would let him court her. A worm of pain slid behind her ribs. No chance.

Melissa sat beside her and patted her hand, which was like getting a strong hug from someone else, and then went back to the library—she'd only come up to use the chamber pot. No doubt more of her secret work with Charles Goddard.

Keri slept like the dead, but when she woke, her first thought was of Val Muffet.

CHAPTER 11

The-man-with-kind-hands was asleep. The-other-man who helped him was asleep too, slumped on a low bed in the corner of the room. She had woken up and played with him in the night. It had been fun.

She was hungry.

The window here didn't have bars.

She worked out how to open it, but the-other-man had stopped her doing that last night. She would wait until he was gone.

In the meantime, she would make a nest from this bit of cloth.

She began to tear it apart. That was fun.

.   .   .

THE NEXT MORNING, though it was so shocking it made her breathless, she knocked on Val's door. Mama had been right, and she would keep him at a distance from now on; but Genevieve still needed to be cared for.

Shepherd, his valet, answered the door, looking decidedly the worse for wear.

Poor man.

"Er...Genevieve?"

"Please tell me you've come to take her away, my lady." The man was almost begging.

"I'm so sorry she's been a trial to you, Shepherd.   We'll   find..er...we'll   find somewhere..."

Val appeared behind Shepherd. She carefully didn't smile at him, and a quick frown went across his face.

"She's gone again," he said. "Climbed out the window."

"She's probably gone to the orchard. She smelled of apples last night."

She and Val ran downstairs together, hoping to slide out the side door without notice.

They never made it. The hall was full of people, all talking at once.

A series of surprises. First, Petroc's engagement to Beatrice, and then, astonishingly, Ives turning up with Katie—*married*!

Forced to marry, because of some silly prank of Ives, kidnapping Den's coach, not realising that Katie was inside, Katie told her in a whispered aside. They *said* it was an elopement, but who would believe that? Katie knew that she wouldn't. If her best friend had been in love, Keri would have known.

Of course, Katie had been compromised beyond recovery. How *awful*!

VAL MADE a discreet exit from the family brouhaha. None of his business. He carried a fellow-feeling for Ives Trengrouse. Not a bad lad, but young to get married, especially if the girl's mother didn't approve of you, which apparently was the reason for the elopement.

Yesterday—Lord, that seemed like years ago! Yesterday, Kerenza had said they'd get the men out to search for Genevieve, but with all this hubbub it was clearly not the time to ask.

Even the children were gathered in the hall, agog at the revelations.

He'd have to search by himself.

Walking to the orchard with a bowl of gooseberries he'd begged from the cook, wishing he could loosen his neckcloth in the warm summer morning, he found himself dwelling on Keri's face this morning. She hadn't smiled at him.

There'd been a definite coolness.

Cold light of day, he guessed. Come to her senses, as his father would say.

That's good, he tried to convince himself. He should be glad, for her sake, that her, her *sweetness* to him had been no more than a temporary companionship forged by their shared care for Genevieve. Damn, she had him thinking of the baboon by name. Devil's daughter, that's what she was.

His heart wasn't in the anger. Poor Genevieve. She had looked so lost and alone last night.

He was in the mood to feel kinship with that.

THE SMALL ONES weren't in the apple trees.

Shame. She liked them.

It was nice here. Warm. Sunny. Green. Quiet.

Very quiet. It was unnerving.

She was used to the rumble of carts and the evening shouts of the-men-in-red at home. The troop all knew the shouts.

'*Halt. Who comes there?*' "*The keys.*' '*Whose keys?*' '*King George's keys.*' '*Pass, King George's keys. All's well.*'

They would hoot along in rhythm and then

laugh and go to sleep. Every night, winter and summer, with the big ravens cawing their annoyance outside the bars.

She missed the safety of that routine. When would her troop leader find her?

Perhaps she should stop escaping. If she stayed in one place, perhaps he would find her.

The-man-with-kind-hands was approaching.

No.

She didn't want to go back to the small room. The troop leader would never find her there.

She would go to the top of the stone mountain and keep watch for him.

HE'D HAD NO LUCK. And worse, as he went up the stairs to his room to wash for nuncheon, his father cornered him.

"Never mind, lad," Pa said kindly. "There's other fish in the sea."

Never mind? Oh. Lady Beatrice and Petroc.

"It's fine, Father. They're well suited." In love was what they were, but one didn't say that. Perhaps this was a good time to push his father on the future. "Come in, Father."

He opened his door. Going by the missing jug on the washstand, Shepherd was getting his hot water. Good. He waved his father to the only chair, and sat on the bed.

Shrewd hazel eyes took in his clasped hands and, no doubt, the serious look he was trying to put on his face. "Well, what is it, lad?"

"Why won't you take me into the business with you? I've no wish to be a gentleman farmer."

Pa pursed his lips consideringly, and then sighed. "Aye, I know. But, lad…you're no businessman either."

What? He'd worked hard at the manufactory. In the office. Even on the floor, when necessary. All right, he didn't have his father's engineering brain, but—

"It's not that you're not a bright lad," Pa hastened to say. "You just don't…you don't *care* about the business. It's not in your blood. Maybe if I'd kept you with me instead of sending you off to that fancy school…" He straightened and firmed his mouth. "You're too nice, lad, that's the problem. Manufacturing is a tough business and you need the instincts of a shark. That's not you."

"You think I'm too soft." He'd heard that often, as a child. Boarding school had toughened him up; but obviously not enough.

Pa ignored him. "You take after my father. A lovely man, he was. The best father I ever saw. But without my mother, he would have gone under time and again. Your mother was the same as mine. Your ma ran the office until her death, you know, with the girls under her feet and the wet-nurse in the corner. Tough as nails." His voice was full of admiration and love. "She's the reason we thrived."

His mother had been, well, absent through most of his childhood. He'd taken it for granted. It was only as an adult he'd realised how unusual it was. When she was around, she was kind. He'd loved her. But it had been her who'd said, "You're too soft," over and over again.

Pa cleared his throat, as though embarrassed. "You need an *instinct*, to succeed in business, lad, and you don't have it. That's why I'm taking Caroline in to manage the office."

Caroline? She was two years younger, and he'd thought her no more interested in business than—well, than he was, deep down. She'd managed the house once the two older girls had married, and done it well, certainly. The managing kind, Caroline.

A weird mixture of desolation and relief swept over him. He hadn't realised how much he'd dreaded walking back into the manufactory, knowing it would be for life. Like a prison sentence. And yet, at least he'd have had a *purpose.*

"So what do I do?"

"We'll think of something." Clearly relieved to have the conversation over, Pa slapped his hands on his thighs and jumped up. "Mebbee ask his lordship."

No. Ask Kerenza father to decide what he was good for? Never.

"Or maybe not."

Pa grunted. "Up to you. We'll discuss it more when we get home."

So that was it? Fine. He had a sudden impulse to disturb his father's evident satisfaction.

"By the way, Pa. That baboon rode our coach all the way here, and we can't find her. We had her in the old dairy, but she escaped."

That shook him.

"*What?*" Then, as shrewd as ever, he homed in on the unsaid part. "Who is "we"?"

"Lady Kerenza. She gave me a place to keep her, but the devil's daughter escaped. Again."

"Nothing better happen to her. The Prince Regent won't be happy. And ye must not disturb the household!" Pa wore his magisterial face, which had often preceded a whipping when he was younger. But he was an adult now.

He wanted to say, "You should have given her to Caroline to look after," but that would be childish.

"I know. She can look after herself. There's too much going on today for a general search, but I'll get the children involved this afternoon."

"Hmph. You've kept this quiet all through the ball? What were you thinking!"

"I was thinking that it was my responsibility."

Astonishingly, that was the right thing to say.

"Aye. Aye, it was. Keep me posted."

Lord. He sat back on the bed, exhausted, as his father left. Too many ups and downs in a short time.

He didn't know if he envied Caroline, or pitied her. She would love it, though. Something to get her teeth into.

Inexorably, it seemed, his thoughts

turned to Kerenza. What would *she* want to do with her life?

He had no idea. He knew the deep aspects of her character—her kindness, her practicality, her love of her family and friends. Yet he knew almost nothing of the surface, except that she liked to dance.

He probably never would know more.

"Goddamit!" He threw a pillow across the room just as Shepherd came back with the hot water.

Shepherd stared at him with some compassion.

"Just so, sir," he said. He put the water down and picked the pillow, fluffing it before he put it back on the bed. "Time to wash, sir? And perhaps a new neckcloth? Sir has a small smudge on that one."

Val bowed to the inevitable. Whatever happened, one's neckcloth must be pristine.

AFTER THE FUSS had died down, Kerenza slid

into Katie's new room (Ives' room—it was so odd!).

"Are you all right?"

Katie turned from the window with tears standing bright in her eyes, and cast herself into Keri's arms.

"We *had* to!" she cried.

"Well, of course you had to. I could just slap Ives! He's so harum-scarum, and look what he's done to you!"

They sat on the bed and Katie cried some more, but then sat up and dried her tears. "No. Ives has been…good. Kinder than I expected. He organised everything so we could be married by the Bishop, which helped Mama deal with it."

Typical of Ives, to skate through a difficult situation through charm and connections.

"But it's so *horrible!* You wanted to marry a lord!"

Katie's blue eyes were bleak. "Mama was determined I would. I just wanted to marry someone I-I loved."

And now she was tied to Keri's madcap of a brother, who wasn't even a baronet. It wasn't fair.

"At least we'll be sisters," she said, hugging Katie. "And we can still have our Season together. Ives couldn't be so cruel as to keep you in the country when the rest of us go up."

But he could if he wanted to.

She thought about that as she readied herself for dinner in their bedroom. Now that they were married, Ives could make any decision he wanted to about Katie's life.

Keri shivered. At least Ives was good-hearted, and they'd known each other all their lives. How was *she* to judge someone if she'd only met them at balls and routs? When they were at their best, with all their faults concealed?

Arranged marriages might at least avoid some horrible outcomes; assuming the parents knew more about the groom than the bride ever could. She did know that Papa had "made enquiries" about John Mandeville before he allowed Demelza to marry him. She'd overheard him reassuring Mama about it, so long ago it felt like another life.

The Season loomed in front of her as a treacherous bog, with so many pitfalls and potential for disaster.

How could a girl make a good decision when she'd never seen anything of life?

Her turn to be put into her evening dress. She wished Melissa was here so she could ask her advice about marriage. Melissa's judgement could always be depended on. But she was off on some errand with Felix and Lion.

Maryann had been with Melissa in her two Seasons in London.

"Maryann!" She turned so Maryann could do up her front ribbons. "Do you think you get to know people during the Season?"

Maryann slid a glove onto her fingers. "In some ways, very well, my lady. In others, not at all."

"That's not helpful."

Her maid bit her lip.

"Ladies are trained up to a particular life," she said, her voice carefully neutral. "It doesn't suit everyone."

"I want that life." Even to her own ears, her voice sounded desolate.

"You can have it, miss, don't you worry. You'll go to London and be a Diamond and a Success, and have dozens of men at your feet. Just as Miss Melissa did."

Keri sighed.

"It'll be all right, Miss Keri," Maryann said in a whisper. "All the young ladies feel nervous before their debut."

Impulsively, she hugged Maryann, and hurried out.

As they walked down the stairs, she realised that she'd never once imagined her life after London. Her first Season, and perhaps the one after that, and a brilliant Society wedding, had occupied all her fantasies. She'd never really thought about married life.

Perhaps Katie had never thought about it either, and now had to face it. Perhaps it took someone like Melissa to see clearly.

CHAPTER 12

The sun was coming up. She couldn't remember ever having seen that.

It made the world feel very big and her very small.

She had waited all night, but her troop leader had not come.

She didn't know what to do next.

"Mama…"

"Mm?"

They were putting the good china away after the festivities. Mama always did it herself, to make sure her precious Sèvres pieces were safely bestowed. The "girls" were helping: Melissa, Demelza, herself—and Katie. Kerenza had taken advantage of a moment alone with her mother, but now she didn't know how to put her question.

"What will Katie do now?"

"What do you mean?"

"Well…will she just live with us forever?"

Mama straightened from arranging the cups and saucers and regarded her with a frown.

"You don't want her to?"

"Oh, of course I do! She's my best friend! But…but what will she *do*?"

"She'll help me, as you do. She's a daughter of the house, now."

"Is that what you did, when you first came here?"

Mama laughed and sat down in the red armchair which was her favourite. "Lud, no! Your father's mother was dead, and I was pitchforked into running this huge house with no time to learn how everything operated. I was lucky to have a good house-keeper, but the butler *hated* me!"

"Carveth?" Surely not.

"No, no. Carveth was a footman then. No, Polkinghorne was the old butler, and he'd been ferociously loyal to his mistress. Thought of me as in "incomer". Which I was. But I certainly had plenty to occupy me! Even the old earl didn't like me much, though he'd chosen me himself!"

Kerenza froze. Her parents were so comfortable together, she'd always assumed…

"Your marriage was arranged?"

Smiling, her mother nodded. "Of course. My dear, it was beyond rare for a girl to choose her own husband in those days. If her parents were indulgent, she might have the choice of two or three, but they would have been carefully selected. No going off to Almack's to eye your options! I never questioned but that my husband would be chosen for me. Indeed, my parents were sticklers… even on his deathbed, my mother called my father "my lord"."

"But you love Papa!"

"My dear, who could not love a husband like him?"

That was odd. She hadn't really answered the question. Kerenza sat on the arm of the chair and hugged her mother's shoulders, a thing Mama frowned upon. But this time, she took Keri's hand as though glad of the contact.

"Are you *happy*, Mama?"

That was the wrong question. Mama shook herself and got up, letting go of Keri's hand.

Then she paused.

"I've been very happy raising my children. Now you're all grown…I'm sure I shall find something else to occupy myself with."

She went out, calling for the next consignment of china from the scullery.

Keri stayed sitting on the arm of the chair; her mother's answer, interpreted, had been: "No. I'm not happy."

Yet it had also been: "I will make myself happy."

She wasn't sure if she should be admiring of Mama, or sad for her. If she, Kerenza, went to London and married a lord, she'd be expected to do what Mama had done: build her life around his estate, his servants and his children.

She'd thought she wanted nothing better.

Yet Mama had *not* said that she loved Papa, which was inconceivable after so many years together.

These past few days, Keri seemed to be seeing the world in an entirely new way. Perceiving things beneath the surface she'd never suspected, like Melissa not wanting to marry.

Perhaps that meant she really was growing up.

She didn't like it.

Almack's and the Season occupied her mind through the rest of the china procession and stowing away. How could you truly know what a man was like, enough to choose to marry him?

Actions spoke louder than words, but if

the only actions you ever saw were dancing and perhaps riding, what on Earth could you learn?

Not like watching someone care for an injured animal. *That* showed who you truly were.

VAL KNEW he had to keep searching for Genevieve, but he deserved some nuncheon first.

Keri was sitting in the breakfast room, the sun through the big windows lighting her dark hair and making her once more look like a Madonna, complete with halo.

He stopped in the doorway, just looking at her.

She gazed back, her mouth poised to say something, her eyes speaking for her.

His feelings were on show too, but he couldn't seem to control that.

Keri got up slowly, and put her napkin down. Her long lashes came down on her cheeks, a flush rising.

A step forward. Two steps. He put out his hand.

"Kerenza…"

She looked up and her eyes were full of tears. It stopped him cold. Only a cad would say something—*anything*—now. Dashing the tears away, she ran out of the room.

Damn. Now he'd made her unhappy, which gave him a corkscrew of pain in his chest.

Godammit.

PERHAPS THE TROOP leader was *inside* the stone mountain! There were many people there, so many she couldn't sort out their scents.

She would look.

She would look and she would find him, and things would go back to the way they should be.

Also, there might be more of the small round yellow things to eat.

· · ·

GENEVIEVE SCAMPERED THROUGH THE HOUSE, jumping from table to sofa, settle to mantelpiece, ornaments crashing in her wake, the housemaid screaming, Bryok shouting, and Val vainly begging everyone to calm down.

She scooted into the dining room, where the china cabinet was.

"My china!" Mama cried, and followed. Val and Keri went after her, and Val closed the door firmly behind them.

The sudden quiet was a blessing. Genevieve was on the long table, brandishing a silver candelabra, chittering.

"Shh, shh," Val said.

Keri went forwards, laying a hand on Mama's arm to keep her still.

"Here, little one," she said soothingly. "It's all right. No one will hurt you."

Genevieve wasn't convinced.

The other door opened, and Papa came through, with Mr Muffet senior, both of them with a hessian sack in their hands.

"Please, sir, stay still!" Val said firmly. Astonished at his tone, they froze.

"If we can all be quiet," Keri whispered, "she might come to me."

Another disturbance outside had Genevieve jumping up and down, baring her teeth.

"Oh, for God's sake, be *quiet!*," Keri hissed.

THE-GIRL-WHO-SMELT-OF-LEMONS was trying to trick her with soft words again. And the-man-with-soft-hands too.

She would NOT be quiet! She had waited, and waited, and she could not find the troop leader, and she was sad and angry and lonely and they had to make it *right*!

Hooting, she swung the shiny thing again. The tall woman screeched. Hah! Yes, be afraid! She was *strong*!

Then someone made a noise outside. WHY did they make so much noise! It wasn't good. It hurt her ears.

Another door opened and the girl's face showed surprise.

Genevieve turned.

Was that–?

It *looked* like the troop leader, but it didn't smell like him. He should smell of animals and hay and food, but this male smelled of oranges and thyme and soap. She hesitated.

"Please stay still," the-man-with-soft-hands said.

"No need for that," the new man said.

It was *his* voice! He *was* the troop leader. She had found him!

She dropped the shiny thing, ran down the table and leaped into his arms, which came up to welcome her.

Chittering her displeasure at being abandoned so long, she hid her face in his coat, as she had done as a little one, and he patted her firmly.

"It's all right, Molly. I've got you now."

Molly. *That* was the right name. She gave out a big sigh, and relaxed into his arms.

It would be good now. The troop leader would take her home.

· · ·

"MOLLY?" Kerenza said.

"And you are?" her mother asked, full of icy politeness.

Val cleared his throat. "Countess, may I present Sir Anthony Hoult. The caretaker of His Majesty's royal menagerie, at the Tower of London."

Oh. Was this good or bad?

Looking at Genevieve (Keri just couldn't think of her as Molly), clearly in seventh heaven and clinging to Sir Anthony like a babe to its mother, she was inclined to think good.

"Sir Anthony," Keri said smoothly, dropping a properly respectful curtsey.

Val caught on immediately, and bowed. "Yes, Sir Anthony. We're so glad you're here."

He was surprised by that, and so was everyone else. She moved forward and placed a hand on Genevieve's back.

"She's been *so* unhappy."

"Yes. Yes, indeed!" His calm demeanour cracked a little. "I had expressly told His Majesty that baboons should *not* be taken away from their troop. They are highly so-cial animals, and pine and–er–" He looked around at the evidence of cracked crockery and dented table. '–are inclined to mischief when they are unsupervised by their troop leaders."

Fortunately, Genevieve decided to for-give her, and nibbled gently on her fingers.

"Does that mean–"

Sir Anthony nodded. "I've come to take her back. I'm sorry, er, miss…"

Mama rallied at that. "Sir Anthony, my daughter, Lady Kerenza. And, this is Mr Muffet." She waved a hand at the two older men. "And his father.

So Mama and Papa knew Sir Anthony. Good. That made it easier. She curtsied again and all the men bowed, even her fa-ther, which just showed how flustered things were.

"The Muffets and I have met," Sir An-thony said. "When they first visited the Menagerie." His tone was frosty, but then thawed a little. "In fact, I received a most interesting letter from a Mr Muffet subsequently…?"

He looked from one to the other, as if unsure which had written.

Val nodded to him, and he nodded back, but that didn't seem to reassure Val.

IT WAS ALL WELL and good to give her back, and God knew he was thankful to be rid of her, but there was still the matter of the Prince Regent's gift.

"But His Majesty–" he said.

"Ah, yes." Sir Anthony dug into his pocket, and produced a sealed packet. "His Majesty, in apology for having to remove his gift, has sent you this. To your father, whom I believe was the original recipient?"

Wordlessly, Val took the packet to his father. It had the royal seal on it. Pa cracked it open and said, "Hah! The Letters Patent." He thumped Val on the shoulder. "Caroline will be beside herself!"

Good for Caroline.

"We still have to give the Regent a gift in return!" he whispered urgently.

"D'ye take me for a nodcap, boy? I gave him a so-called loan the next day. Came down handsome, too. It was clear he didn't want a set of tinware!"

Sir Anthony pretended not to notice that exchange.

So he'd been worrying for nothing. Val went back to Sir Anthony and Keri. And Genevieve—er, Molly.

Now that she was going, he was curiously sorry to see her leave. He patted her on the back and, to his astonishment, she leant out of Sir Anthony's arms to rub her head against his.

"Hmmm. She seems to have taken to you. That's quite unusual."

"He's been *wonderful* to her!" Keri was always so passionate. It was one of the things he loved about her. One of the things he would miss.

"I have convinced the Prince Regent to plan a new menagerie. A zoological gardens, as part of this new Regent's Park John Nash is talking about. I shall be needing a promising young man to be my assistant and to take over in good time. I trust Molly's instincts. And the ideas in your letter had real insight. I could use someone who cares about animals and has ideas." He fished his card case out and gave Val a card. "If you're interested, come and see me when you're next in London."

What an astonishing prospect!

Sir Anthony bowed as best he could to the earl and countess, nodded at the rest of them, and took his leave.

They were left standing there, amazed, Pa and the earl hanging on to the now-useless sacks.

"Well!" the countess said.

"This is *wonderful!*" Keri said, grabbing his arm. "Assistant Head at the Royal Menagerie. Working for the Prince Regent directly!"

Oh. Yes. He supposed it *was* rather wonderful. He felt rather as though he were in one of those fairy stories where everything suddenly changes from ordinary to magical. Or perhaps the other way around.

Building a new menagerie. Yes, that *was* something he could get interested in. A real purpose. And it would be engrossing for Keri...

He looked up at Earl Trengrouse. Keri's hand was still on his arm, and the old man was staring at it fixedly. Pre-Genevieve, he would have hastily moved away, but the last few days had tempered his metal. He stayed still.

"I daresay," the countess said, "that Sir Anthony will want you to live at the Tower, as he does." She paused and stared at the earl meaningfully. "That's quite a respectable address."

Keri was frozen, but she smiled at the earl hopefully.

"Perhaps I may call on you when you remove to London?" Val suggested it in as airy a voice as he could muster, as though it were a mere bagatelle, instead of the most important question he would ever ask.

The older men exchanged glances, and Pa threw his eyes to heaven, shrugging. The earl took in a long breath, and let it out.

"You may," the earl said. "Leave your card when you arrive, and we shall invite you to dinner."

Keri flew down the room and hugged her father. "*Thank* you, Papa!"

"I make no promises!" the earl added hastily. "And I'll have no clandestine engagements! He can come to call, and we'll see from there." He harrumphed.

"Yes, Papa."

She smiled back at Val and he felt his soul light up with happiness. There would be one more question, an even more important one, but that could wait.

They were in no hurry.

EPILOGUE

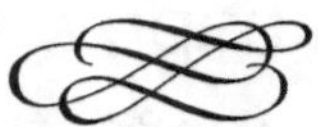

ll was well. The troop leader had brought her home, and she was safe and happy with her troop around her, snuggling at night in the cold winter, jeering at the lions until they swished their tails, hooting at the parrots and the ravens every morning. Life was in its accustomed round, and it was good.

Also, the-man-with-soft-hands was living here too, which was good, because the-girl-who-smelt-of-lemons also came often, and brought the little yellow foods which tasted so good. Molly knew the name now: custard tarts.

Sometimes the troop threw food at the people who came to stare, but they never threw the custard tarts.

Molly liked seeing the man and the girl together. They looked happy.

And when they were together, there was more food.

MORE FROM ELIZABETH LEYDIN

I hope you've enjoyed the fourth book in the Trengrouse Ball series. There are more–see below.

Sign up for Elizabeth's Substack blog, 'Corsets & Coaches', where she shares true-life Regency stories and tidbits, as well as news about her latest releases, or watch her "This Week in the Regency" videos on Youtube.

More Trengrouse Ball Sweet Regency Romances

The Trengrouse Ball books can all be read as stand-alones – the timelines overlap, but each story is separate.

The Captain and the Lady
Book 1 in the Trengrouse Ball series

Petroc Trengrouse has come home from Waterloo missing his right leg.

Family friend Lady Beatrice Marlowe has been thrown out of her home on the deaths of her father and brother.

When Petroc comes to stay at Beatrice's mother's seaside house to recover from his wounds, he has no idea that he's causing severe financial problems.

He feels he's not fit to marry; she knows she's too poor to attract an aristocratic suitor. Will the Trengrouse Ball prove both of them wrong?

The Youngest Son
Book 2 in the Trengrouse Ball series

A heart-warming, forced marriage friends-to-lovers romance.

When Ives Trengrouse hijacks his friend Den's coach after the Trengrouse Ball, he thinks it's no more than a prank. But Den isn't inside. Instead, it's his sister Katie, going home early with a migraine.

Compromised beyond saving, the two must marry immediately—and do so. Katie's dreams of a big London Season are gone. Ives can't go on his light-hearted, care-for-nothing way now he's a married man.

Neither of them wants to be in this marriage: can they turn childhood friendship into something deeper?

Second Chance at Christmas
Book 3 in the Trengrouse Ball series

A heart-warming second chance Christmas story.

Widowed, pregnant Lady Demelza Mandeville returns to her family home, Trengrouse Hall, after her husband's recent death, dreading meeting family friend, Sir Denzell Kelynack, who jilted her in her first Season.

Denzell looks forward to the meeting—he wants to know why Demelza had jilted him eight years ago. And what role did his needy, unstable mother play in that?

Finding out the truth, and finding a path to a new life, is complicated by Demelza's pregnancy. If the baby is a boy, she'll be bound to the Mandeville estates until he's an adult; if a girl, she's free to live her own life while a Mandeville cousin inherits the estate.

The Trengrouse Ball is a promise of things to come, but will the promise come true at Christmas?

My Earl, the Spy
Book 5 in the Trengrouse Ball series

An exciting ace romance with a twist of espionage!

Lady Melissa Trengrouse can't imagine being married to anyone but Charles Goddard, Earl of Westholm, for whom she decodes secret French dispatches.

Although she hates the idea of marriage or children, for Charles, Melissa would endure it all. They're perfect for each other: but when she proposes to him at the Trengrouse Ball, he refuses her without explanation.

Charles has his reasons. He hates hurting her, but it's a relief when he has to ride off on a secret mission for the Crown.

Melissa realises he's riding into a trap. Can she save him and discover his secret reasons for denying that he loved her all along?

A sweet Regency romance with an atypical couple!

The Lion and Miss Lamb
Book 6 in the Trengrouse Ball series

Sarah Lamb doesn't have a family; Endellion Trengrouse has never fit in with his.

Immediately attracted, the two have a brief flirtation at the Trengrouse Ball, which ends disastrously when Endellion—known as Lion—finds out the truth behind Sarah's birth. Sarah isn't surprised by his reaction: she knows no respectable man will marry an illegitimate orphan.

But there's more to Sarah's parentage—and Endellion's—than either of them know. Can they find the truth…and will that truth bring them together, or drive them apart?

This story first appeared in the Sweet Daughters of Duke Street series.